My Girls & Curls

Layla Steele

Illustrated by Renata Smagulova

Young Authors Publishing

Young Authors Publishing
www.youngauthorspublishing.org

Book Design by April Mostek

Our books may be purchased in bulk
for promotional, educational, or business use.
Please contact Young Authors Publishing by email at
info@youngauthorspublishing.org.

Dedication

To my mom who is always looking out for me, supporting me, and pushing me to my best.

Today is Lila's birthday

and to celebrate, her friends Ashley and Sarah are going to the pool with her. Lila's mom is driving the girls to the pool and Ashley gets compliments about her new silk press.

Lila says, "Ashley your hair is so nice!"

Sarah agrees, "I love your hair! I see you, girl!"

Ashley thanks both of her friends.

Ashley normally gets a silk press for special events and Lila's birthday was just that.

After they get dressed in their swimsuits,

the girls head to the pool to kick their feet in the water. Lila brings up the idea of having a fashion show when they get back to her house and both girls agree!

The Atlanta sun was beating down

on the girls' backs so after a little while, the girls grabbed each other's hands and jumped in the pool. The water felt so good!

When Ashley comes up from the water,

her silk press becomes a mini afro. Ashley feels bad because it took so long to get her hair straight! Even though she is sad, she doesn't tell her friends because she didn't want to ruin their pool day.

Ashley runs to the bathroom

and looks in the mirror. She sees her natural curls looking fluffy like cotton candy and as big as clouds. Ashley's mom always did her natural hair, so Ashley didn't know what to do for the fashion show!

The girls get in the car

and Ashley finally explains to them why she's feeling upset.

"My hair is ruined!" cries Ashley. "My hair is all curly and tangled again!" Sarah and Lila knew what they had to do.

As soon as the girls get home, Sarah and Lila begin to think of ways they can help Ashley with her hair. Ashley's curls are beautiful, but they knew she wanted a change in her hair style.

Sarah says that there is a new hair style app that can show you how to do different natural hairstyles. Lila loves this idea. "Yeah! Let's do it!" she says.

Lila and Sarah

grab the hair products, brushes, and combs while Ashley looks in the mirror, still sad about her hair.

Sarah starts by giving Ashley two cornrows

going straight back and cute, swooped edges. Ashley asks to go look in the mirror to see if she likes it.

Ashley didn't like the braids,
so Lila tries giving her space buns instead.

Ashley still doesn't like her hair

and she begins to cry! Lila and Sarah feel so bad for their friend and want to make her happy again.

Ashley wants to try one more hairstyle

her mom always does with her hair. She shows Lila and Sarah a picture and Lila knows how to do the style.

Lila parts Ashley's hair in half

and gives her a bun at the top while the back is left in curls.

Ashley goes to the mirror and exclaims, "I love it! It's perfect for me!" She is ready for the runway.

The girls finish up and they are ready for the runway. Everyone feels confident and beautiful in their skin with their stylish hair.

Ashley learns that her natural hair is beautiful in whatever state it's in. Thanks to the help of her friends, she now knows that she can conquer anything. Lila says, "This is the best birthday ever!"

About the Author

Layla Steele, 9, is a student in elementary school who is passionate about singing, drawing, and playing video games. The daughter of a supportive, yet crazy mother, Layla enjoys talking to her friends and expressing herself through fashion. She loves being around her family, especially her younger cousins. She hopes this book inspires them, and her readers, to love their hair and always be confident. Layla is currently starting her own business, Blue Paradise, creating affordable perfumes.

ABOUT YOUNG AUTHORS PUBLISHING

We believe that all kids are story-worthy!

Young Authors Publishing is a children's book publisher that exists to share the diverse stories of Black and Brown children.

How We're Different

Young Authors participate in a 1-month 'Experience Program' where they are paired with a trained writing mentor that helps them conceptualize and write their very own children's book. Once their manuscript is completed, our young authors attend workshops to learn the fundamentals of financial literacy, entrepreneurship, and public speaking in an effort to ensure they have the tools they need to succeed as successful published writers. Young Authors Publishing is on a mission to empower the authors of tomorrow, using their words to change the dialogue around representation in literature.

Learn more about our impact at
www.youngauthorspublishing.org

YOUNG
AUTHORS
PUBLISHING